*Dear Parent:*
*Your child's love of re*

D0571427

Every child learns to read in a diffe _____ .. ... own speed. Some go back and forth between reading levels and read favorite books again and again. Others read through each level in order. You can help your young reader improve and become more confident by encouraging his or her own interests and abilities. From books your child reads with you to the first books he or she reads alone, there are I Can Read Books for every stage of reading:

**SHARED READING**
Basic language, word repetition, and whimsical illustrations, ideal for sharing with your emergent reader

**BEGINNING READING**
Short sentences, familiar words, and simple concepts for children eager to read on their own

**READING WITH HELP**
Engaging stories, longer sentences, and language play for developing readers

**READING ALONE**
Complex plots, challenging vocabulary, and high-interest topics for the independent reader

**ADVANCED READING**
Short paragraphs, chapters, and exciting themes for the perfect bridge to chapter books

**I Can Read Books** have introduced children to the joy of reading since 1957. Featuring award-winning authors and illustrators and a fabulous cast of beloved characters, I Can Read Books set the standard for beginning readers.

A lifetime of discovery begins with the magical words **"I Can Read!"**

*Visit www.icanread.com for information*
*on enriching your child's reading experience.*

The Chronicles of Narnia®, Narnia® and all book titles, characters and locales original to
The Chronicles of Narnia are trademarks of C.S. Lewis Pte. Ltd. Use without permission is strictly prohibited.

HarperCollins®, 🖋®, and I Can Read Book®
are trademarks of HarperCollins Publishers.

Prince Caspian: This Is Narnia
Copyright © 2008 by C.S. Lewis Pte. Ltd.
Art/illustration © 2008 Disney Enterprises, Inc. and Walden Media, LLC.
Printed in Italy.
No part of this book may be used or reproduced in any manner whatsoever without written permission
except in the case of brief quotations embodied in critical articles and reviews.
First published in the United Kingdom in 2008 by HarperCollins Children's Books
HarperCollins Children's Books is a division of HarperCollins Publishers, 77-85 Fulham Palace Road,
Hammersmith, London W6 8JB
www.harpercollinschildrensbooks.co.uk
www.icanread.com
www.narnia.com
ISBN: 978-0-00-725837-6
1 3 5 7 9 10 8 6 4 2
Book design by Rick Farley and John Sazaklis

# I Can Read!

READING 2 WITH HELP

## -THE CHRONICLES OF- NARNIA

### PRINCE CASPIAN

# This Is Narnia

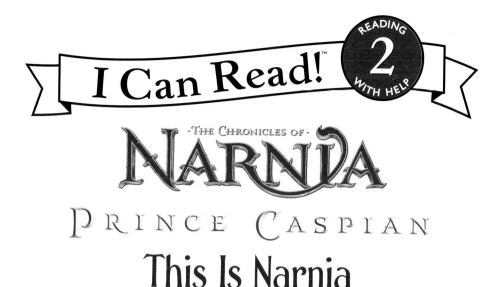

Adapted by Jennifer Frantz

Based on the screenplay by Andrew Adamson &
Christopher Markus & Stephen McFeely

Based on the book by C. S. Lewis

Directed by Andrew Adamson

HarperCollins*Childrens Books*

The Pevensie children

waited for their train.

WOO-WOO!

A horn sounded.

But this was not the train horn.

It was a magic horn,

calling the children.

In a flash,

the Pevensies

were in a magical land.

It was Narnia!

Narnia was an amazing place.

Animals could speak.

Trees could dance.

And time went by very quickly.

The children
had been here before.
Once they ruled Narnia
as Kings and Queens.

Now Susan, Peter, Lucy and Edmund
were in Narnia once again.
They were by a sparkling sea.

The Pevensies played in the water.

Then they stopped to look around.

The children saw an old castle.

"I wonder who lived there?"

Lucy asked.

"I think we did," said Susan.

"Cair Paravel!"

said Peter.

That was the name

of their old castle.

The Pevensies went inside.

They found their old clothes

and other things they had left behind.

Cair Paravel used to be beautiful.

It was once full of life.

But now it was different.

Where were the magical creatures?

Lucy thought of her old friends.

"They're all gone," she said sadly.

The children had to find out

what was going on.

The Pevensies

reached a river.

Suddenly, they saw

someone in trouble!

Soldiers had a Dwarf tied up.

"Drop him!" said Susan.

She drew her bow and arrow.

The soldiers dropped the Dwarf

and ran away.

The Dwarf was named Trumpkin.

He was a Narnian.

Peter helped him to the shore.

"I'm King Peter," he said.

"You're the Kings
and Queens of old?"
Trumpkin said.
"We were hoping
for someone who could help us."

To prove his skill,
Edmund challenged
Trumpkin to a sword fight.
Before the Dwarf could move,
Edmund had won.

"Beards and bedsteads!"
Trumpkin said in surprise.
Maybe these really were
the old Kings and Queens!

Trumpkin told the children
what had happened
since they left.

"Telmarines came," he said.

These greedy humans

had invaded Narnia.

The evil Telmarine ruler
wanted to be King.
He wanted to rule all of Narnia
and its creatures.

The only hope for Narnia
was the ruler's nephew,
Prince Caspian.
Caspian was a kind Telmarine.

But Prince Caspian was in trouble.

His evil uncle

wanted to get rid of him.

So Caspian had run away.

Caspian was the one
who had sounded
the magical horn for help!

It was up to the Pevensies

to find Prince Caspian

and help him save Narnia.

Trumpkin agreed to help.

So they set off on their adventure.

Their task would not be easy.

Many things had

changed in Narnia.

But Lucy, Susan, Edmund and Peter
would still do anything
for this magical land
they loved so much.